SQUAWK 7500

Terrorist Hijacks Pacifica 762

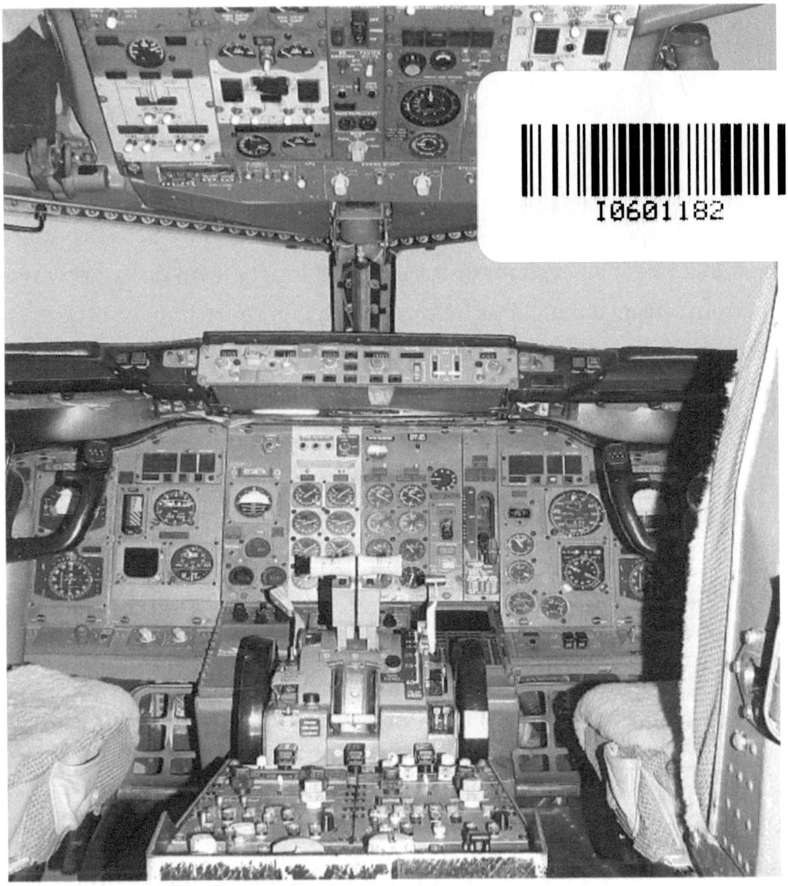

I0601182

Captain Steve A. Reeves

TotalRecall Publications, Inc.

www.totalrecallpress.com

TotalRecall Publications, Inc.
1103 Middlecreek
Friendswood, Texas 77546
281-992-3131   281-482-5390 Fax
www.totalrecallpress.com

Copyright © 2008 by: Steve Reeves

ISBN: 978-1-59095-844-5
UPC 6-43977-58844-9

Printed in the United States of America with simultaneous
printings in Australia, Canada, and United Kingdom.

FIRST EDITION
1   2   3   4   5   6   7   8   9   10

TO Stacy, Keegan, and Kayleigh
You are the wind beneath my wings

September 26, 2008

Author's Words

This fiction thriller is based on the real life experiences of a commercial pilot and gives you an exciting insider view of what it takes to fly a jet while managing crew, passengers

—and a terrorist!

Captain Mike Rendell started out his workday like all the workdays before – just another normal day of flying. After spending a raucous night partying with his crew, he and his first officer were looking forward to a nice relaxing flight to the West Coast.

"Flaps 1, climb power", Mike repeated as he responded to the command of Gary Ellis, his new-hire First Officer. Mike positioned the flap lever from the "5" spot to the "1" spot and retarded the thrust levers to approximately eighty-eight percent of full power. This was the standard "after take-off" configuration and gave the aircraft its' best rate of climb in relation to burning the least amount of fuel. Pacifica Airlines Flight 762 had just departed from Chicago's Midway Airport. On board the Boeing 737 were 137 passengers, three flight attendants, and two pilots.

However, it didn't take long for events to unfold that would thrust Captain Rendell and his crew into one of the most terror-filled days of their commercial airline careers. The lives of his flight attendants and his passengers hung in the balance as Mike battled the elements, a deranged passenger, and aircraft malfunctions as he attempted to bring his fully loaded jumbo jet in for a safe landing....

Table of Contents

Saturday
0645 Central Standard Time

May 24th

It wasn't uncommon for Mike Rendell to hit the snooze button three or four times before he mustered up the energy to face the day. But today he was wide awake before the alarm made its first chirp. Turning on the bedside lamp, Mike rolled out of bed and reached his arms toward the ceiling. Oh, yeah, the stretch felt good! He did a couple of jumping jacks and a few torso twists and set down on the edge of the bed.

Picking up the bedside phone, he pressed the number that connected him directly to room service. Told that the kitchen staff wasn't busy and that his breakfast could be delivered right away, Mike placed his order and hurried to the shower. Amazingly, just as he had finished drying off, the room service waiter knocked on his door. Mike was amazed because, normally, his days away from home did not run this smoothly.

Usually his alarm clock malfunctioned, there wasn't any hot water, or room service would take forever to deliver his order of cold eggs and even colder coffee.

The ultimate injustice, however, would be some punk pulling the fire alarm at three o'clock in the morning, waking Mike from a sound sleep with only two hours remaining before he actually had to get up. But today none of that happened. It was surreal. Perhaps, during the night, the sun, the moon, and the stars had all lined up in a perfect orbit followed by nature and mankind falling into flawless harmony. Suddenly, Mike had a "flashback", recalling the old, toothless fortune-teller who had told him once that sometimes the juxtaposition of the planets are but a thin veil concealing unexpected troubles. But he softly chuckled and shook his head as he pushed that portentous thought aside and with a smile in his heart, and contentment in his soul, sat on his bed, Indian-style, eating his breakfast and flipping the TV between ESPN and The Weather Channel.

After Mike had eaten his hot and hearty breakfast all that remained of his morning rituals was for him to brush his teeth, comb his hair, and don his dark blue pilot uniform. Standing in front of the hotel room mirror and softly humming an old Eagles' tune - Hotel California - Mike was finally able, after two bumbled tries, to fashion a presentable knot in his tie. A quick three hundred sixty degree turn in front of the mirror convinced him that the rest of his tailored uniform was in tip-top appearance.

Returning to the main area of the suite, Mike scoured the room for any items that he may have overlooked while packing. Not finding any stray socks or wandering underwear, he zipped up his roller bag and set it by the door. He walked to the desk and, as he was picking up his wallet, a credit card receipt fluttered to the carpet. It was a pleasant reminder of the raucous crew party that had taken place last night in a local pub. As a smile crept across his face, Mike crumpled the paper and shot it into the wastebasket. Gazing at his watch, he saw that he had fifteen minutes until he was required to catch the airport shuttle. Plenty of time to call his wife before he started another average day of flying an airliner cross-country.

Mike pushed the speed dial number on his cell phone. As his wife, Lisa, picked up the kitchen phone, she was greeted with a "hey, babe" from her husband of 13 years. She responded with a wifely "hey, you", and then said, "we need to talk before you take off."

"OK, shoot."

"After I drop the girls at school, I'm going down town to run some errands. Do you still want me to pick up the tickets to the football game or will you do it when you get home?"

"Well," Mike said, "since the ticket office is only twenty minutes from the airport, why don't I pick them up on my way home tomorrow?"

"Excellent," Lisa said. "That will save me some time today." Pausing briefly, she asked, "Do you want to say 'good morning' to the girly-whirlies before I take them to school?"

Mike took a quick glance at his watch. "Sure," he said. "I've got a couple of minutes."

Mike briefly talked to each of his two girls; Sara, who

was in fifth grade and Holly, who was in second grade. He made them promise that they would pay attention in class and eat the nutritious lunch that their mother had packed for them. The girls told their dad that they loved him and they would see him when he got home. Mike told them that he loved them, too, and to put their mother back on the phone because he was starting to run late.

"Hey," he said to Lisa, "I'll give you a call tonight when I get to Seattle."

"OK, babe. Take care and be safe. Love ya!"

Mike hung up the phone, picked up his bag, and walked out of the room. When Mike reached the hotel lobby, he could see that the rest of his crew, the first officer and the three flight attendants, had already checked out and were helping the van driver load their bags. He placed his key on the counter and walked through the double front door. Placing his bags with the others, he glanced up at the sky. "Man, what a beautiful day for flying," he thought. Mike put his sunglasses on and climbed in to the passenger's front seat.

As the courtesy van pulled away from the hotel's awning and was bathed in the early morning sun, Mike Rendell, forty-nine year old captain for Pacifica Airlines, was looking forward to starting another typical day of flying – totally oblivious to the fact that old, toothless fortune-tellers were occasionally wiser than they looked.

Saturday
0944 Central Standard Time

"Flaps one, climb power."

"Flaps one, climb power," Mike repeated, as he responded to the command of Gary Ellis, his new-hire First Officer. Mike positioned the flap lever from the "5" spot to the "1" spot and retarded the thrust levers to approximately eighty-eight percent of full power. This was the standard "after take-off" configuration and gave the aircraft its' best rate of climb in relation to burning the least amount of fuel. Pacifica Airlines Flight Seven Sixty-Two had just departed from Chicago's Midway Airport. On board the Boeing 737 were one hundred thirty-seven passengers, three flight attendants, and two pilots.

The flight had originated in Cleveland, with a stop in Chicago, before terminating in Seattle, Washington. Mike had informed Gary, during the push-back in Cleveland, that he would take this leg even though, according to the rotation, it was Gary's turn to fly. Mike explained that he didn't feel a new-hire First Officer, especially one with limited time in the Boeing 737, possessed the necessary skill level to not scare the shit out of him while the "newby" attempted to land on Midway's notoriously short runway. His reluctance to let Gary land at Chicago was based on historical perspective. Mike had been a First Officer for three long years before a Captain gave him a shot at a Midway landing.

However, the same restrictions did not apply to departures. Gary had executed a flawless take-off from Runway 4R and was at the controls of the Boeing. Mike was working the radios. It was a stunningly clear morning in the Windy City as both pilots constantly scanned the horizon, keeping a vigilant look-out for aircraft that were lining up to land at the other downtown airport, Meigs Field.

There were numerous boats on Lake Michigan; most of them sailboats taking advantage of the favorable winds. The combination of white canvas sails, deep blue water, and piercing sunlight compelled both pilots to reach for their Raybans. Just as Gary leveled the aircraft at their assigned three thousand foot altitude, a female voice with a pleasant Midwestern accent came through the pilots' headset.

"Pacifica Seven Sixty-Two, have a good day, gentlemen, and contact Chicago Center on frequency 132.75."

"Pacifica Seven Sixty-Two switching to Chicago Center on 132.75, good day," Mike responded.

Mike dialed the appropriate frequency into the primary communication radio.

"Chicago, good morning, Pacifica Seven Sixty-Two, level at three thousand."

Another female voice responded but this one wasn't quite as pleasing as the previous controller.

"Pacifica Seven Sixty-Two, turn left to a heading of two seven zero. Climb and maintain flight level one eight zero."

Mike acknowledged the clearance and set the assigned heading and altitude in the flight management computer. Gary engaged the autopilot and applied climb power to the turbofan engines. The Boeing, in response to the autopilot inputs, started a shallow climbing turn to the west. As O'Hare airport slipped under the nose, the navigation computer indicated 1,698 miles remaining to Seattle-Tacoma International Airport. Only three hours and twenty minutes until Mike could log another average day as an airline pilot.

Unfortunately, Mike and his crew had no way of knowing that life-threatening events were unfolding in the cabin. Pacifica Seven Sixty-Two would not make it to Seattle today.

Saturday
1004 Central Standard Time

Pacifica Seven Sixty-Two reached 18,000 feet and leveled off.

The ride was smooth and the sky was mostly clear with just an occasional puffy cloud here and there. The corn and soybean fields of Illinois stretched to the edge of the western horizon. Mike reached up to the overhead panel and turned off the "Fasten Seatbelt" sign. He then selected the "Public Address" position on the auxiliary radio panel. Picking up the hand-held microphone next to his right knee, Mike delivered the customary "Welcome Aboard" speech, telling the passengers how much the airline appreciated their business, the weather forecast for the destination, and the expected time of arrival. Having completed that task, he replaced the microphone and ensured that his headset and transmit button were back in the primary radio position. Within seconds, the unpleasant voice of the Chicago controller was back in his ear.

"Pacifica Seven Sixty-Two, you are clear of O'Hare inbound traffic, climb and maintain flight level four zero zero, and you are cleared direct to Seattle-Tacoma International."

"Roger, Pacifica Seven Sixty-Two is climbing to flight level four zero zero and cleared direct to destination," Mike replied.

Mike dialed the new numbers into the flight management computer while his First Officer monitored the autopilots' climb and slight course correction. He took a quick glance at the load sheet that the Operations Agent had handed to him back at Midway Airport. Immediately he noticed that the aircraft was still a little too heavy to reach 40,000 feet. Mike pressed the transmit button on the left side of his yoke.

"Chicago Center, Pacifica Seven Sixty-Two is too heavy to reach flight level four zero zero. For performance purposes, we are requesting flight level three two zero as our final cruise altitude."

Since no other aircraft were flying at that altitude,

Chicago Center granted his request. Mike decreased the altitude in the flight management computer from 40,000 feet to 32,000 feet. The aircraft was currently climbing through 29,000 feet and in just a couple of minutes would reach its assigned altitude. All of the computers and navigation radios were working correctly so Mike loosened his seat belt, slid his chair back, and tried to make himself comfortable for the long flight ahead. With nothing vitally important to do, he began reminiscing about last night's party.

"Who was that cute girl you were dancing with last night?" Mike laughingly asked his First Officer.

Gary shrugged his shoulders and said, "What are you talking about?"

Loosening the knot in his tie, Mike laughed a little harder.

"Don't play ignorant with me. I saw you on the dance floor hugging that cute brunette."

"Oh, that girl!" Gary replied. "Man, I never did get her name; as a matter of fact, I don't think she even knew what her name was! She'd been downing Hiroshimas like they were going out of style, and I wasn't hugging her, - I was trying to keep her from falling down!"

'Hiroshima' is the name of the house specialty drink of the *Bombs Away Pub*. Loaded with a witch's brew of hard liquors, anybody foolish enough to drink an entire mug would feel like they had been instantly vaporized. The pub is a favored hang-out for the local airport workers and flight crews overnighting in nearby hotels. It is shaped like a Quonset hut straight out of a World War II movie. Patrons enter the establishment through a series of above-ground tunnels constructed of olive green sandbags and old wooden planks. Drop lights, connected by bare electrical conduit, are strung from the planks every ten feet to light the way. Speakers, mounted at the top of the tunnel, blare a continuous loop of bombs exploding and the rat-a-tat-tat of machine gun fire. Approaching the entrance, the big band sounds of Tommy Dorsey, Cab Calloway, and Glenn Miller can be heard leaking through the front doors. Once inside, the cavernous interior is stuffed with the requisite battle-scarred military paraphernalia, including a full-scale P-51

Mustang fighter swooping down from the ceiling. The walls are covered in camouflage netting of various colors and textures, and the tables have vintage Air Corp squadron and Army unit patches laminated to the top of them. A bar, imported from an English pub, is located adjacent to the entrance and a small wooden dance floor, bordered by more sand bags, is situated in the far corner of the building. The wait staff is costumed in various styles of WWII military garb – the bartenders have the choice of wearing a sailor or soldier uniform, the hostesses wear tailored replicas of bomber pilot uniforms, and the waitresses wear white mini-skirts, low-cut white blouses, and a white nurse's cap with a red cross printed on the front.

The previous evening, Mike had led his first officer and flight attendants into the *Bombs Away Pub* to have dinner and drinks. It didn't take long before they realized the place was crawling with other Pacifica pilots and flight attendants. Sensing the perfect opportunity for a crew party, Mike herded the crewmembers to the back of the pub where they joined together several tables. As the "nurses" brought the pitchers of beer, Mike made his way around the tables, saying "hello" to the pilots that he knew and introducing himself to the ones that he didn't. Everybody was laughing at the latest company gossip which mostly pertained to certain pilots and flight attendants observed "hooking up" at the various crew hotels. The frothy pitchers were being delivered at a constant interval and a festive atmosphere, along with the jitterbug beat of Louis Jordan's "G.I. Jive", permeated the pub.

As the party progressed, Mike and several pilots eventually migrated to one end of the conglomerate of tables. It wasn't long before the "only by the grace of God have I lived this long" stories started flying fast and loose. This tradition dates back to shortly after the bicycle brothers from Dayton stunned the world at Kitty Hawk. These frightening tales usually start with the pilot/storyteller finding himself in some sort of dire straits only to survive by employing his superior knowledge and flight skills. It is truly a professional pilot that can keep a straight face during the recitation of these heroic accounts, because all aviators, from the freshly soloed student pilot to the most senior commercial airline pilot, know that "pilot stories" are ninety-nine percent balderdash topped with one percent bullshit.   Or vice versa, depending on the number of cocktails consumed!

Mike wasn't much of a "party animal" so, around 2100 hours, he started saying his farewells. The party was in full swing and several flight attendants tried to talk him into one more "Charleston" before he left. But Mike wanted to get back to his room and check in with his wife and daughters. Tomorrow was a school day; if he hustled he could talk to his daughters before they went to bed. Mike told the flight attendants that he appreciated the offer but he really had to go. He promised them a "rain check" for the next time that they met. On his way out of the pub, he cornered their waitress and paid the tab for the entire table. Mike made his way through the pub, waving good-bye to those that were out of hearing range. As he took one last look around before entering the tunnel, he noticed his first officer on the dance floor, slow dancing with a cute brunette - both hands on her butt and whispering into her ear.

"So you were just trying to keep her from falling down? Yeah, right!" Mike said as he winked at his first officer. He was letting Gary know that his answers were scoring high points on the bullshit meter.

"No, really! Things aren't always what they...."

Ding. Ding. The cabin service phone interrupted Gary.

Mike picked up the phone and said, "Hey."

Saturday
1045 Central Standard Time

Karen Schumacher had been at Pacifica for eleven years.

She never intended to be with the airline that long. Karen had applied for a flight attendant job because it looked like it would be fun and exciting. But it wasn't going to be her life's work. She studied fashion design at San Diego State University on her days off and, as soon as she had her degree in hand, she was off to the Big Apple to make her mark in the Garment District. However, during the summer, between her junior and senior year, she volunteered to work a charter flight to St. Louis, unaware that her future soul- mate was sitting in the first officer's seat.

An intense courtship ensued, followed by a brief engagement that culminated in a lavish wedding held the same week that she graduated from SDSU. The nuptial was attended by practically every flight attendant and pilot at Pacifica Airlines.

That was nine years, and two kids, ago. Karen's husband is now a captain, she is a senior flight attendant, and the Garment District is a fading memory. She still considers her job "fun" even though she occasionally feels guilty leaving the kids at home without their mommy.

Karen was standing in the aft galley, facing the service door, when Mike answered her call.

"Mike, we have a male passenger in the back that is starting to cause trouble for the people sitting around him."

Mike was dumbfounded and slightly perturbed by the vagueness of her declaration.

"What do you mean by 'causing trouble'?" he asked her.

For some reason that Mike couldn't understand, Karen answered him in a whisper.

"He's becoming very combative toward me and the other girls. Also, he's kicking the seatback in front of him and screaming profanities at the other passengers."

"Where is he now? Is he moving about the cabin or messing around in the galleys?"

Again, Karen answered in a whisper, "Right now he's

still in - gotta go!"

The line went dead.

Mike removed the handset from his ear, briefly looked at it, and then placed it back to his ear.

"Karen? Karen?" he said into the phone.

There wasn't any response so Mike slowly hung up the phone. He folded his arms across his chest and appeared to be falling into a deep trance.

Gary had monitored the phone call from his set of radios.

He looked at Mike and, with a quizzical tone in his voice, said, "I wonder what that's all about?"

Mike continued sitting motionless. Gary thought that perhaps he hadn't heard him so he was getting ready to ask his question again when, suddenly, Mike bolted upright in his seat.

"Where are we?" he asked Gary.

Both pilots obviously knew that they were somewhere between Chicago and Seattle but neither knew their exact location. Gary selected the "Present Position" page on the flight management computer. The computer indicated that the aircraft was at the assigned altitude, flying the correct heading to their destination, and passing over south-central South Dakota. Mike let out a groan as he looked at the computer screen.

"What's the matter?" Gary asked.

Mike responded, "I have a sneaking suspicion that our day is getting ready to take a turn for the worse. And if you look at the charts, you'll notice there aren't any airports in this part of the country that can handle a heavy jet. Damn!"

Gary asked, "What makes you think we might have to find a landing spot out here?"

"Well, I don't know for sure. It's just that I've been around long enough to get these funny feelings whenever bizarre stuff starts happening. And a flight attendant hanging up the way she did is definitely bizarre. In eighteen years of flying, I've never had that happen!" Mike thought for a second and then continued, "Let's complete the FFDO checklist and then I'm going to contact the company."

Both pilots had been trained by the Transportation Security Administration to be Federal Flight Deck Officers, licensed to carry a handgun while at work and authorized to use deadly force to defend the cockpit. Mike and Gary ensured that their semi-automatic 9mm pistols were in the proper position. They discussed the possibility that the strange behavior of the passenger may be an attempt to take the flight attendant's attention away from the cockpit door. It was agreed, that if a breach of the door occurred, Gary would defend the cockpit with all of the deadly force available and Mike would assume control of the aircraft. Neither pilot cherished the thought of actually killing anybody but, after the tragedy of 9-11, both of them were acutely aware of the consequences of allowing a terrorist into the cockpit.

With the cockpit security checklist complete, Mike thought it best to inform the company of his current situation. On the forward portion of the center console is a device called "ACARS". Its function is to allow pilots and their dispatch office to send airborne e-mails to each other. Mike sent an e-mail to his dispatcher telling him that the senior flight attendant had called to report an abusive passenger in the cabin and he would send additional information as it became available. Several minutes later the reply from dispatch arrived – "roger, keep us advised."

Mike had printed a copy of the message from Dispatch and was storing it in the flight case behind his seat when Gary said, "Mike, check this out." Whatever it was, Mike knew from the tone of Gary's voice, that it wasn't going to be good. Mike locked the flight case and raised his head.

Just visible on the horizon, a hundred or so miles away, were the blossoming tops of a line of thunderstorms stretching from Canada to Colorado. Mike stared intently at the approaching weather and said, "Damn! Those weren't in the forecast."

Saturday
1105 Central Standard Time

Alternating his attention between the cockpit's radar scope and the approaching weather, Mike reached up to press the flight attendant call button. He needed to inform Karen that a line of thunderstorms were approaching and he wanted her to update him on the situation in the cabin. However, before he could press the button, the service phone rang – ding...ding. Expecting Karen's whispery voice on the other end, he picked up the phone. But Karen wasn't whispering. She was downright joyous.

"Mike, I think we have everything under control now!"

Mike was relieved to hear that his very capable senior flight attendant had kept a fist-fight from breaking out in the cabin.

"What happened?" he asked her.

"Well, like I told you, this guy just started acting really weird. He was hollering profanities at people seated in his aisle and, occasionally, he would kick the seat back in front of him which, you can imagine, really upset the guy sitting in the seat. Anyway, I brought him back to the aft galley and gave him a soft drink and some pretzels which seems to have calmed him down."

"That's great Karen; nice job," Mike said. "I want you to keep an eye on him and try to get him back in his seat. We're just crossing the border between South Dakota and Montana and I really don't want to land out here in the boonies if we can avoid it. However, if he starts acting up or you absolutely can't deal with him anymore, we'll do what we have to do."

"OK, Mike, I'll keep you posted. Believe me, I'm not in any mood to babysit a grown man all the way to the…"

Mike heard Karen scream, "I have to go!"

The connection was lost.

Mike replaced the phones' receiver, looked at his pistol, and moved his finger to the radio's transmit button.

Saturday
1110 Central Standard Time

"Chicago Center, Pacifica Seven Sixty-Two, request."

"Pacifica Seven Sixty-Two, Chicago Center, you're flying out of my airspace now. Contact Denver Center on frequency 124.55 with your request."

"OK, Denver Center on 124.55, Pacifica Seven Sixty-Two, see ya," Mike replied as he jotted down the new frequency.

Karen's scream and rapid hang up of the phone had rattled the cockpit's peace and tranquility. Both pilots knew that the flight was going to terminate – and very shortly. It was now up to Mike, as the pilot in command, to figure out "where" and "when".

Aware that the aircraft was crossing into Montana and, coincidentally, having just returned from a family vacation in the state, Mike knew that Bozeman and Billings each had small airports. With a lot of finesse and a little luck, he might be able to get their sixty-ton aircraft stopped on one of their short runways. Mike checked in with Denver Center.

"Denver Center, Pacifica Seven Sixty-Two, flight level three two zero, request."

"Pacifica Seven Sixty Two at flight level three two zero, Denver Center, good morning, go ahead with your request."

"Sir, we have a situation developing in the cabin and we need the current weather in Bozeman and Billings."

As Mike released the transmit button on his radio, another airliner, not waiting for an appropriate pause in the conversation, checked in on the frequency and, in the process, blocked Denver Center's acknowledgement of Mike's request.

Showing his irritation with the rudeness of the other pilot, Denver Center told him to standby and said, "Pacifica Seven Sixty-Two, we are pulling up the weather in Bozeman and Billings. I'll get back to you in just a minute."

While Mike had been talking to the controller, Gary had opened the divert kit and had located the charts for both airports. Utilizing the Onboard Performance Computer, and factoring in the aircraft's current weight, it was evident, from the data spit out by the computer, that it would be extremely "iffy" getting the jet stopped on either airport's runway. He handed a print out of the landing data to Mike.

Mike took the print out and placed it on the window glare shield. He instinctively knew that the sheet of paper did not hold any good news and right now he had something more important to do. He wanted to know, right now and without a doubt, what in hell was going on in the cabin. Mike picked up his phone and called the aft galley. He listened to it ring … and ring … and ring. No one answered. He hung up and called the forward galley. No one answered there, either. Suddenly, the voice of Denver Center came through his headset.

"Pacifica Seven Sixty-Two, Denver Center, sorry about the wait. Advise me when you're ready to copy the Bozeman and Billings weather."

"Go ahead, Denver," Mike said as he picked up a pen and paper.

"The Bozeman weather, at the top of the hour, was sky overcast with a three hundred foot ceiling, the wind is out of the north-northwest at fifteen knots, gusting to twenty knots, and the visibility is three-quarters of a mile in light to moderate snow. The Billings weather is the same except the ceiling is variable between three hundred and four hundred feet. Do you copy?"

Mike and Gary looked at each other with an expression of utter dismay bordering on shock. Neither one of them was very excited about the prospect of diverting a fully loaded Boeing 737 in to an unknown airport, located in mountainous terrain, with a blowing snow storm in progress. Not to mention that the odds of getting one hundred twenty thousand pounds of airliner stopped on a slick runway were slim and none. Mike was silently cursing under his breath when he heard it …

Ding. Ding.

Mike jerked up the phone, "Karen, I need to know what's going on with that passenger," he yelled over the line.

Except it wasn't Karen on the other end.

"Mike, this is Michelle."

Michelle was the "B" flight attendant, working in the aft section of the cabin. Michelle was a perky blonde who had entertained the crews at last night's party by placing a quarter between her butt cheeks, standing over a brandy snifter placed on the floor, and accurately dropping the coin into the snifter from a standing position. The entire pub broke into wild applause each time she "bombed" the wine glass.

"We've got a major, major problem back here! The guy that Karen's been talking to you about – he just went ballistic! He has Karen pinned up against the aft service door and he's squeezing her neck! And, Mike, he's telling me to tell you to take him back to Chicago." She paused. "Hold on, he's yelling at me. He wants me to tell you something else."

Mike could hear some muffled voices as Michelle placed her hand over the phone. Within a few seconds she was back on the line.

"Mike, he's telling me that he has a knife and if you don't turn the airplane around he's going to kill Karen and everybody else on the plane!"

Mike couldn't believe his ears. This kind of stuff didn't

happen to him! And who, in their right mind, let this psycho through airport security?

"Michelle, are you hurt? Is Sabrina hurt?"

Sabrina was the "C" flight attendant, working in the mid-cabin area. A devoutly spiritual woman, she had not bothered to attend last night's party.

"No, I'm not hurt and I don't see Sabrina! I think she's up in the forward cabin area, keeping an eye on the cockpit door!"

Mike could tell that Michelle was starting to hyperventilate.

He gave her a couple of seconds before he asked, "Michelle, are any of the passengers helping you?"

"No!" Michelle said as she tried to control her breathing. "They're all cowering in their seats! Wait. I see a young boy walking back this way!"

"Good," Mike said. "Now, Michelle, do you see the knife?"

"No, I don't see the knife! He has his left hand on Karen's throat and the other hand in his front pocket!"

Mike would never forget what happened next.

Michelle screamed, "Oh, my God, Mike!   I have to go! Get us down quick!"

The line went dead.

Saturday
1155 Central Standard Time

"Denver Center, Pacifica Seven Sixty-Two, Mayday."

The communications between the controller and the other aircraft abruptly ceased and the reply from Denver Center was instantaneous.

In a shocked voice, the controller said, "Pacifica Seven Sixty-Two, say again!"

Before Mike could respond, Gary pointed at the radar screen and said, "We need to do something about this line of thunderstorms."

Mike had become so preoccupied with the safety of the flight attendants and the marginal weather in Bozeman and Billings that he had lost track of the thunderstorms looming ahead. "Damn. Like I don't have enough trouble already," he thought.

While Mike was trying to determine their next course of action, Gary piped up, "When I was flying corporate jets from Canada, we always cleared U.S. Customs in Great

Falls. Maybe we should take a look at their weather since it's about the same distance from here to Great Falls as it is from here to Bozeman or Billings."

Gary was a new first officer at the airline but he wasn't a new pilot. A graduate of Spartan School of Aeronautics, he had spent the last ten years flying corporate jets all over the world and, just recently, started dabbling in aerobatics. No fewer than twenty-five Pacifica pilots had recommended him for employment when his resume came up for review. His suggestion would turn out to have a significant impact on the flight.

In the background, both pilots could hear the Denver controller say, "Pacifica Seven Sixty-Two, if able, repeat last transmission or squawk appropriate code."

"Squawk appropriate code" was the controllers' way to discreetly ask the pilots if they were being hijacked or had some other type of emergency that, for some reason, couldn't be mentioned over the radio. Pilots are able to non-verbally communicate with air traffic controllers by setting specific numbered codes in the transponder, a device on the aircraft that is "pinged" by the ground based radars. The squawk code for "hijack" is 7500. Once a radar scope detects a 7-5-0-0 code on an aircraft, bells ring at the controllers' station and several emergency procedures start taking place. Mike instructed Gary to set 7500 in the transponder, then pressed his transmit button.

"Denver, Pacifica Seven Sixty-Two, we have a hijack in progress and I'm declaring an emergency at this time," Mike said into his microphone. Again the response from the controller was instantaneous.

"Roger, Pacifica Seven Sixty-Two, we copy and we see your squawk. Say your intentions and, when able, sir, I need your aircraft type, fuel on board, and number of souls on board."

A flash of lightening illuminated the cockpit as Mike responded, "OK, Center, I'll get all of that in just a second but right now I have an urgent request."

"Go ahead with your request," Denver came back.

"Sir, I have a line of thunderstorms at twelve o'clock and approximately twenty miles. I need a block clearance for a cruise altitude of eighteen thousand feet through forty-one thousand feet. Also, I need multiple course changes of plus or minus forty-five degrees for weather avoidance, over."

Denver Center replied, "Roger, Pacifica Seven Sixty-Two, we are in the process of clearing all traffic out of your airspace and putting a ten mile 'no fly zone' around your aircraft. You are cleared as requested."

"Roger, stand-by for the additional information that you requested," Mike said as he glanced over at Gary.

Another bolt of lightning, brighter than the last, filled the cockpit as Mike instructed Gary, who had disconnected the autopilot and was hand-flying the aircraft, to fly whatever course and altitude needed to stay out of the thunderstorms. Mike was extremely concerned with the possibility of encountering turbulence. The last thing he wanted to do was bounce a flight attendant, or helpful passenger, off the ceiling of the aircraft. Gary was in a climbing right turn to skirt a rain cell, leaving Mike free to concentrate on finding a suitable place to land. And Mike needed to land – quickly.

"Denver Center, Pacifica Seven Sixty-Two, I need the

current weather report for Great Falls and be advised that we are executing multiple deviations for thunderstorms and moderate rain showers."

The controller must have been reading the captain's mind because he started reciting the Great Falls weather as soon as Mike had released the radio transmit button.

"The current Great Falls weather is, ceiling one thousand five hundred feet, visibility is greater than ten miles, and the wind is out of the southwest at seven knots. The active runway is runway twenty-one, over."

Finally, some good news! Great Falls airport was reporting weather conditions suitable for Mike to execute a visual approach and, from the charts that Gary had placed on the center console; the runway was long enough for them to land. Mike looked over at Gary who, although starting a left turn to keep clear of another thunderstorm, was pumping his arm up and down like he had just hit a homerun. There was no need for further discussions between the pilots – Great Falls was the new destination.

Mike keyed his transmit button. "Pacifica Seven Sixty-

Two is requesting a clearance from our present position direct to Great Falls International Airport."

"Pacifica Seven Sixty-Two, you are cleared as requested."

Saturday
1216 Central Standard Time

Gary tried to make an immediate turn for Great Falls but was blocked by an intense rain cell. He made a sharp turn away from it and pulled up on the nose of the aircraft in an attempt to climb above the more destructive area of the storm. The past fifteen minutes had been mentally and physically exhausting for him.

Constant turns – left, then right - and multiple climbs and descents had taxed his stamina. But, so far, he had been able to maintain a fairly smooth ride and, according to the display on the weather scope, once he cleared this rain cell the worst part of the weather would be behind them and he could set a course for Great Falls.

Seeing that Gary was doing a brilliant job of flying through the holes in the line of thunderstorms, Mike decided to call the cabin. Again, no one answered. He then rang the special code which requires a flight attendant to drop whatever he or she is doing and immediately answer the phone. There was no response.

Mike's thoughts briefly turned to the passengers he had spoken with at the gate in Chicago; the senior couple on their way to visit their first grandchild, the young woman smiling over a very large and pregnant belly who asked him to explain "cabin pressure", and the mother sending her unaccompanied minor son to Seattle to spend his seventh birthday with his father. He wondered how they were coping with the horrifying situation in the cabin. The fear and anxiety in Karen's voice and in Michelle's screams resounded again and again in his mind. The mental image of one of his crew, helpless and with a knife to her throat while a madman threatened to kill everyone on the plane, was a scene from his worst nightmare. Mike's wife had been a flight attendant before they decided she should stay home with their daughters – little girls the same age as some of the children that he had seen board the plane. The thought of his wife fighting a knife-wielding lunatic was unbearable. Mike shook the image out of his head and turned to his first officer.

"Gary, as soon as we get through this weather, we're going to run the engines all the way to the red-line. We'll back off a little on the power when it looks like they're about to throw a fan blade. I want this jet going so fast that it peels the paint off."

"You got it, boss. By the way, it looks like this little storm cell passing behind the right wing is the last of the heavy weather."

Mike glanced at the radar screen. Sure enough, the weather returns indicated on the radar panel were changing from red, to yellow, to finally a dark green. The aircraft lurched forward as Mike pushed the throttles to their full forward position. It didn't take long for the engines to stabilize at their maximum power output which resulted in a constant, but light, vibration as the aircraft reached its "redline" airspeed.

At thirty-six thousand feet, Pacifica Seven Sixty-Two was hurtling through the troposphere at five hundred fifty miles per hour. The navigation computer indicated three minutes until the descent point was reached and estimated seventeen minutes until the aircraft touched down at Great Falls International Airport. Mike and his first officer clipped the approach charts to their control yokes and oriented themselves to the layout and surrounding terrain of the airport.

Having punched out of the line of thunderstorms, the aircraft was flying in nothing more than light drizzle. The ride was mostly smooth but Mike turned on the seatbelt sign anyway and made an announcement to the cabin that they were landing very shortly. Hoping that the clouds had sufficiently masked their true location, he didn't mention where they were landing. His plan was to get the plane on the ground, as quickly as possible, and let the authorities take it from there.

As the descent point was reached, Gary smoothly lowered the nose and started down. Mike rang the cabin for the third time. For the third time, there was no answer. He switched his transmitter selector back to the main radio panel and broadcast, "Denver Center, Pacifica Seven Sixty-Two, request." Again, the response was instantaneous.

"Pacifica Seven Sixty-Two, yes, sir, go ahead with your request."

"Confirm that you have notified Great Falls law enforcement and all appropriate agencies of our emergency status."

"Pacifica Seven Sixty-Two, affirmative, Great Falls law enforcement is standing-by at the airport. Also, be advised that we've been in contact with your dispatch office and they're aware of your location and intentions, over."

Mike had been too busy to send an ACARS message to the dispatch office. He told the controller that he appreciated his assistance.

The controller said, "No problem, sir. And while I have you, would you please give me your specific aircraft type, fuel on board, and SOBs."

"Roger, Denver, we are a Boeing 737, we have two hours plus fifty minutes of fuel on board and we have one hundred forty two souls on board; one hundred thirty-seven passengers plus five crew. And I have another request."

Denver Center responded, "Thank you, sir. I copied all

of that. Go ahead with your request."

Mike took a deep breath and held it for a couple of seconds. Not being able to contact the flight attendants had led to ominous thoughts. Thoughts that weren't pretty. Nonetheless, he had to be prepared.

"Yes, sir," Mike replied, "I need you to confirm that we will have medical personnel available to meet the aircraft."

"Pacifica Seven Sixty-Two, can you give me some idea as to how much medical attention you will require upon arrival?"

Mike exhaled and said, "Denver, I have one hundred thirty-seven passengers on board and I haven't been able to contact any of my flight attendants for the past twenty-two minutes. The last I heard from the cabin, one of the girls was being held, at knifepoint, by a male passenger who stated he was going to kill everybody on the plane. I'm not aware of any injuries at this time; however, the situation could be extreme. Please have as much medical assistance standing-by as you possibly can."

There was a short pause as the controller mentally

processed the scene Mike had painted for him.   The controllers' solemn response was barely audible in the pilots' headsets.

"Pacifica Seven Sixty-Two, roger, sir.   We'll get all the medical personnel that we can."

Saturday
1225 Central Standard Time

Denver Center issued Pacifica Seven Sixty-Two a descent clearance to sixteen thousand feet.

Mike re-engaged the autopilot while the pilots reviewed and briefed the arrival and landing in Great Falls. Gary, the first officer, would fly; Mike would work the radios and coordinate with airport ground personnel and the law enforcement officers.

The aircraft had flown out of the drizzle so Mike switches the radar from the "weather" mode to the "ground mapping" mode. Although they were in thick clouds and couldn't see a thing, the ground mapping screen indicated the mountainous terrain that surrounded them – the higher elevations in red, the intermediate in yellow, and the lower in green. The controllers have the same mapping mode on their radar scopes; it is their responsibility to assign headings and altitudes that will keep aircraft clear of the high terrain. Mike's equipment is merely a backup but it was comforting for the pilots to "see" the invisible mountains that passed silently beneath the wings. Approaching sixteen thousand feet, the controller contacted the crew.

"Pacifica Seven Sixty-Two, Denver Center, continue your descent to ten thousand feet, turn right to a heading of zero three zero; vectors for a left downwind to runway 21, and contact Great Falls approach control on frequency 118.55."

"Pacifica Seven Sixty-Two, roger, sir, we copied all of that, good day and thanks for your assistance."

Denver Center answered in the same solemn voice that the pilots had heard earlier.

"Good day, sir and…good luck."

Mike reached toward the radio panel …

TRAFFIC! …TRAFFIC!...CLIMB!...CLIMB!

Both pilots flinched and instinctively grabbed their control yokes as the piercing alarm of the Traffic Collision Avoidance System blared through their headsets and over the cockpit speakers. They immediately focused their attention on the TCAS screen located at the bottom of the flight instrument panel.   Two fast moving aircraft, represented by the red diamond shapes on the screen, were rapidly closing on them from their twelve o'clock position.

TRAFFIC! TRAFFIC! CLIMB! CLIMB!

The pilots have twenty seconds until impact.

"Pacifica Seven Sixty-Two, Great Falls Approach, disregard any TCAS warning you may be receiving, sir."

The TCAS system screamed even louder as the time until impact reached ten seconds.   The pilots must execute an immediate six thousand foot per minute climb to avoid hitting the unidentified aircraft.

TRAFFIC! TRAFFIC! CLIMB! CLIMB!

It took every ounce of mental strength for Mike and Gary to override their primal urge to yank back on the control yoke.

"Pacifica Seven Sixty-Two, I say again, disregard TCAS warnings. Be advised that two Montana Air National Guard F-16's are joining up on you and will escort you into the terminal area."

Due to the cloud cover, the pilots never saw the fighters rocket past their wingtips. However, the aural warnings stopped and the two red diamond shapes on the TCAS screen turned to green once the computer sensed that the F-16s' were no longer a collision threat. Mike released his white-knuckled grip on the control yoke and started breathing again. He should have anticipated the intercept from the fighters since a fighter escort is one of the many security procedures put in place after the terrorist attacks of September, 2001; attacks that started with hijackings.

The Boeing 737 was just a few minutes away from landing. Still in light drizzle and fog, Mike couldn't see the airport but the navigation computer indicated that it was at the twelve o'clock position and ten miles away.

Mike was becoming more anxious as the airport got closer. With no word from any of his flight attendants, and unable to determine the exact conditions in the cabin, he desperately wanted to get the aircraft on the ground as quickly as possible. It was his fervent hope that he wasn't flying a commercial airliner full of bleeding men, women, and children.

The approach controller gave the pilots a heading to line up with the runway. Mike instructed Gary to start slowing the aircraft so they could configure for landing. Their airspeed of three hundred fifty knots was so great that if the landing gear was lowered, or the flaps extended, the wind pressure would tear off the gear doors or rip the flaps off the wings.

With the speed brakes extended and the aircraft slowing to approach speed, the airliner was descending to its initial approach altitude. Two thousand five hundred feet...two thousand four hundred feet, the fog is starting to lift...two thousand three hundred feet; Mike heard his co-pilot gasp and instantly looked up from the instrument panel.

The captain couldn't believe what he was seeing. In twenty-two years of flying, Mike had never observed anything like the scene that filled the windscreen!

Saturday
1242 Central Standard Time

Great Falls International Airport is located on the high plains of Montana; west of the confluence of the Sun and Missouri rivers and surrounded by the Highwood, Little Belt, Big Belt and Front Range of the Rocky Mountains. Although the distant vistas are breathtaking, the airport itself is surrounded only by parched soil and scrub juniper trees. Without the trees, it is reminiscent of an airdrome sitting on the surface of the moon.

However, the scene that filled the pilot's windscreen was not of a distant lunar landing field; rather, that of an airport hanging from the middle of the most brightly decorated Christmas tree imaginable. The pulsing and revolving emergency lights of no fewer than sixty police cruisers, fire engines, and ambulances bathed every square foot of the airport. The vehicles were on the taxiways, the inactive runways, and the ramp areas next to the terminal. Like strobe-fitted ants, a caravan of more emergency vehicles could be seen moving along the airport's perimeter roads. The blinking effect from the thousands of rainbow colored lights instantly added to the headache that Mike had developed shortly after Karen's call to the cockpit. The reflection of the lights on the wet pavement, remaining from the showers the flight had just flown through, increased the surreal visual effect of the "Christmas tree" where the pilots were preparing to land.

"Pacifica Seven Sixty-Two, you are cleared for a visual approach to runway 21."

"Roger, cleared for the visual approach to runway 21," Mike acknowledged.

Gary called for the landing gear to be extended and the reading of the "Before Landing" checklist. Mike lowered the landing gear handle, removed the laminated checklist from the holder on the glare shield, and started calling out the "before landing" items. It was a "command and response" checklist; each item that Mike called out, Gary would confirm the particular flight control, or switch, corresponding with that item was in the proper position.

The checklist was proceeding smoothly until they reached the "landing gear" section – that's when the panic set in.

"Pacifica Seven Sixty-Two, you are cleared to land, emergency equipment and personnel standing-by."

Mike was too busy handling a major cockpit malfunction to verbally acknowledge the controller's clearance. Both pilots were alarmed to discover that the landing gear had not come down when the landing gear lever had been lowered. Pacifica Seven Sixty-Two was ninety seconds from touching down with a malfunctioning landing gear and possibly cartwheeling into the ambulances, fire trucks, and police cruisers lining the runway.

Mike shouted at Gary, "Keep flying – I'll take care of the gear!"

Moving faster than he had ever moved in the simulator, where he semi-annually practiced emergency drills, Mike quickly opened the landing gear access door at the base of the center console and pulled all three manual gear-release levers. The aircraft flight manual states that it takes fifteen seconds for the gear to free fall into position. Mike wasn't sure if that was believable or not. All he knew for sure is they were fifty feet in the air and twenty seconds from either landing or crashing.

Twenty feet. Ten feet. Five feet ... touchdown!

Mike and Gary brace for the impact that was sure to follow – but it didn't happen. The landing gear held; safely down and locked. A joyous feeling immediately came over both pilots but it was short-lived. More trouble loomed ahead.

Gary was having trouble keeping the aircraft tracking down the center of the runway. Like a disco ball from a 1970's era nightclub, the thousands of rotating lights from the emergency vehicles filled the cockpit and practically blinded him. The situation wasn't any better for Mike but it was his responsibility, as the captain, to assume control of the steering once the aircraft was safely on the ground.

Mike swiped Gary's hands off the throttles and said, "I've got it!"

Mike squinted and did his best to battle the blinding lights as he raised the thrust reverse levers and slammed them full aft. The pilots were immediately thrown forward, against their seat belts and shoulder harnesses, as the Boeing jet reacted to a one hundred eighty degree reversal of its thrust vector.

As the airliner rapidly decelerated, and the extreme airframe vibrations, caused by the reverse thrust, began to subside, both pilots were instantly shocked to hear a simple tone reverberate throughout the cockpit - Ding. Ding.

Saturday
1250 Central Standard Time

Mike stowed the thrust reversers since they had done their job of slowing the aircraft's speed to below eighty knots and were no longer effective. The taxiway was approaching to his left so he increased the brake pressure on the rudder pedals in order to not overshoot the turn off. With the engines out of reverse thrust, the noise level in the cockpit dropped dramatically.

Ding...Ding...Ding...Ding.

Mike steered the airliner off the runway and on to the taxiway that leads to the emergency parking area. He could hear the ground controller saying something through his headset but he tuned out the voice. The only person Mike wanted to talk to was the flight attendant that just called him but, first, he told Gary to bring up the flaps and start the auxiliary power unit so he would be able to electrically power the aircraft when he shuts down the engines. Picking up the phone, Mike was bombarded with Michelle's animated voice.

"Mike, we got him down! We got him down!"

The shock of hearing Michelle's voice gave him such a sense of relief that, for an instant, Mike couldn't speak. Finally, he blurted out, "what do you mean 'you have him down'?"

"Do you remember I told you there was a boy coming back to the galley when I had to hang up the phone? Well, the boy, Sabrina, and I started talking to the guy while he's holding Karen. The reason we didn't answer your calls is because he said he'd hurt Karen if one of us picked up the phone. Anyway..." Michelle took a moment to catch her breath. "Anyway, when you turned the aircraft on to the final approach, he saw all of the flashing lights and I think it scared him because he let go of Karen and stared through the galley door window. He had his back to us so Sabrina hit him in the head with a coffee pot and we all jumped him!"

Mike heard the ground controller trying to raise him on the radio so he told Gary to tell the controller that they had finally established contact with one of the flight attendants and the captain would get back to him in a second.

Mike was flabbergasted. Only the spitfire flight attendants of Pacifica Airlines would take on a crazed hijacker with a coffee pot! He continued his conversation with Michelle.

"Are you and the other girls OK?" he asked.

Michelle, her voice an octave higher than normal, responded, "Oh, yeah, we're fine! Karen's a little shook up but she's telling me that she'll be fine. I think she's more ticked-off than anything else. Probably a good thing she doesn't have one of your pistols – she looks mad enough to plug the guy between the eyes!"

"Where's the hijacker?" Mike asked.

"He's hog-tied; lying back here on the floor. Every once in awhile he'll holler and spit and curse. But he isn't going anyplace. Not with two sets of flex cuffs on him."

"OK," Mike said, "here's what I want you to do. I want you to secure the aft entry door slide. I'll have the police come onboard, through that door, when we get stopped up here at the end of the taxiway. Can you handle that?"

"Absolutely," Michelle said, "but, first, we'll have to kick this jerk out of the way."

Mike chuckled as he switched his attention back to the ground controller. Before he called him back, he told Gary to connect the aircrafts' electrical busses to the auxiliary power unit because he was getting ready to shut down one of the engines. Gary shot him a "thumbs up" and started positioning the appropriate switches.

Mike keyed his transmit button, "Ground control, Pacifica Seven Sixty-Two, sorry for the delay, sir, but I've just got off the phone with the flight attendants and they are advising me that the hijacker is secured in the aft galley and there doesn't appear to be any major injuries."

"That's great news, sir," the controller replied, "I'd still like for you to taxi straight ahead to our bomb dispersal area. Law enforcement will meet you there. Also, will you still require medical attention?"

"I don't believe we'll need medical attention on the level that's present," Mike responded as he looked at the dozens of ambulances sitting in the terminal area, "however, I would like to request that we reserve a few ambulances just in case we have an unknown problem."

"Very good, sir. I'll pass that request to the appropriate people."

"By the way," Mike said, "inform the law enforcement officers that I am shutting down the number one engine, that's the engine on the captain's side of the aircraft, and I've instructed the flight attendants to disarm the emergency slide on the aft entry door. I'd like for the police to enter through that door when we get stopped in our parking spot."

"Pacifica Seven Sixty-Two, I will pass your instructions to our security personnel."

With the hijacker tied up and his flight attendants unharmed, Mike began to relax a little. However, the advantageous turn of events did little to relieve his sense of mental and physical exhaustion. Mike felt like he was getting too old for this degree of excitement.

The aircraft was five hundred yards from the designated

parking spot and was still being escorted by several dozen police cars and fire trucks. Gary finally commented on the "light show."

"This is one of the wildest parades I've ever been in," he chuckled.

Mike was starting to agree with his co-pilot's assessment of the activity swirling around them, when he caught a glimpse of a vehicle that was noticeably removed from the crowd.

About three hundred yards down the taxiway, and facing perpendicular to their line of travel, was the most dilapidated pick-up truck that Mike had ever seen. Attached to the rear trailer hitch of the four-wheeled wreck was a set of vintage 1940's air stairs; similar to the ones seen in old Bacall/Bogart movies. It was even possible to make out the old faded Pan Am logo on the balcony rails. However, the most striking and awe-inspiring feature of the air stair and pick-up truck combination was the five FBI SWAT officers crouched at the top of the stairway landing. Each officer wore a black helmet, goggles, a ski mask covering his face, and a black tactical vest with all sorts of pockets and straps. They each carried a short, stocky, black machine-gun. Mike wondered what would happen next.

The SWAT team pulled out of their parking spot as Pacifica Seven Sixty-Two taxied past. Due to the limited visibility in the cockpit, Mike lost sight of them when they passed behind the left wingtip. He assumed that they would follow from behind the aircraft and be in position to board the aircraft once it came to a stop at the bomb dispersal area. However, within seconds of losing sight of the SWAT team, amber warning lights lit up the cockpit indicating that the aft entry door had been opened. Mike continued taxiing, all the while thinking one of the girls had cracked open the door a little too soon.

Approaching the bomb dispersal area, Mike saw a young man, with orange batons, waving him in the direction of his parking spot. It wasn't easy for him to follow the instructions because the flashing lights from the fire trucks, ambulances, and police cars continue to obstruct his vision. Finally, the ramp agent gave the "stop" signal. Mike set the parking brake and shut down the remaining engine. Gary retrieved the parking checklist from its holder on the glare shield and began calling off the items as Mike placed the cockpit switches in their proper position.

With the cockpit secure, Mike removed his headset and released his seat belt and shoulder harness. He could feel the fatigue in his bones as he lifted his body out of his seat.

After sitting on his butt for three hours, it took a few moments for the feeling to come back to his legs. Once his equilibrium was stabilized, Mike opened the cockpit door; he needed to check on his flight attendants.

To his absolute surprise, he was met with thunderous applause from the entire cabin. The grandfather that he had met in Chicago was giving him a "thumbs up" from his third row seat. Sabrina, the "C" flight attendant was on the public address system, asking people, unsuccessfully, to please remain seated until further notice. When she had finished her pleading, Mike called her over.

"Are you OK?" he asked her.

"Yeah, we're OK, but, personally, I don't want to go

through that again!" she said.

"Where's Karen and Michelle?"

"They're in the back, talking to the FBI agents. You won't believe this but, as we were taxiing, the SWAT team pulled up in that old truck and boarded us through the aft entry door."

"Wait a minute! They did that while I was taxiing?"

Sabrina was getting wound up. "It was amazing", she gushed, "You should have seen it! We were in the galley, keeping an eye on that idiot; when, all of a sudden, they pulled up and the aft entry door flew open! The SWAT guys jumped in like a swarm of black ants!"

"What did they do with the hijacker?" Mike wanted to know.

Sabrina calmed down a little bit. "Well, I thought they were going to just hold on to the guy until we got stopped, but they picked him up, all hog-tied, and threw him on to the landing of the airstairs."

Mike was still having a hard time believing what he's hearing so he asked again, "While we're still taxiing?"

"Oh, yeah! They were in, and then out, in just a few seconds!"

"So, they've already gone?"

"Yes," Sabrina said, "But the airport people pulled the airstairs up to the aft entry door and there's a guy back there dressed like a lumberjack who says he's the head of the FBI office."

"Wow," Mike thought.

He took it for granted that a SWAT team would be good but he had no idea that they would be that good.

Saturday
1315 Central Standard Time

Mike stepped back into the cockpit to send an ACARS message to the dispatch office. He typed the following note and pressed the send button:

> *"...safely on the ground in Great Falls.*
> *Crew/Aircraft/Passengers OK. Hijacker in custody."*

Moments later the reply came back:

> *"Great job, Mike. Weather charts and flight plan for*
> *Seattle will be faxed when you are ready to resume*
> *flight operations."*

Mike exited the cockpit and tried to make his way back through the cabin to check on Karen and Michelle. His path was impeded by the well-wishing passengers in the forward section of the aircraft. Glancing over the shoulder of an older lady that had stopped him and wrapped him up in a bear hug, Mike locked eyes with the pregnant girl that he'd spoken with in Chicago. She had a smile on her face but appeared to be wiping tears out of her eyes. She mouthed "thank you" to Mike as the old lady continued to squeeze the air out of him. Mike winked at her and the young mother-to-be started laughing; a stress-releasing laugh that would last several minutes.

Continuing down the aisle, occasionally being stopped to shake a hand or receive a slap on the back, Mike couldn't help but notice two peculiar acting men sitting mid-cabin, each on the opposite side of the aircraft. One looked to be about forty years old, the other slightly younger. They had dark hair, beards, and their faces were shielded by the baseball caps and wrap-around sunglasses they wore. There was a tremendous amount of chatter and conversation taking place in the aircraft; people were engaged with their seat-mates, travel companions, or using their cell phones to call friends and relatives. Yet, these two men, uncharacteristically, sat emotionless in their seats, staring intently out the windows.

Mike finally reached the back of the aircraft and, as he made his way around the aft galley bulkhead, he came face-to-face with a stoutly built man wearing cowboy boots, jeans, and a blue flannel shirt. Mike thought, "This must to be the "lumberjack" that Sabrina mentioned."

The man held out his hand and said, "Frank Edward Cauley, FBI."

Mike introduced himself and then asked the agent, "Where's our hijacker?"

Agent Cauley informed Mike that the hijacker was being taken to the local jail where he'd be charged and booked. The agent then joked with Mike about his casual appearance, noting that he had been at this son's violin recital when he received the call to come to the airport.

Mike quizzed the FBI agent about the massive number of police cars that had swarmed them on their arrival. He was particularly interested in the idea behind the pick-up truck and the airstairs.

"We train extensively for this kind of event, thinking that it will never happen out here in the sticks," the agent said, "however, when we learned that an airliner was inbound with a hijacker aboard, every cop in the state of Montana tried to get here before you landed. As far as the pick-up truck is concerned, that's something we've been toying with for a few months. Our initial trials indicated that it would work under the right circumstances. Today looked like the right circumstance, so we employed it against your aircraft and it worked. By the way, the guys on the truck appreciated you shutting down the left engine. Makes their job a helluva lot easier if they're not fighting the exhaust blast from a big turbofan."

Mike told Agent Cauley that he admired the courage and dedication of his team and he wished that he had been able to see the apprehension of the hijacker in person. Agent Cauley was in the process of responding when his phone rang. Putting the phone to his ear, he turned and walked down the stairs that had been placed against the aft service door entrance. Mike followed and, as he reached the bottom, was greeted by a paramedic.

"Sir, I just wanted to tell you that we've met with your passengers and none of them are hurt; however, a few people are complaining of headaches. We're taking care of those people now. We should be out of the aircraft in just a few minutes."

Mike thanked him for the update and made his way toward the front of the Boeing where Agent Cauley was standing with a black-clad SWAT officer. Mike overheard the officer tell Agent Cauley that the bomb-sniffing dog had cleared the cargo compartments and the bad guy's luggage had been removed. The agent thanked the SWAT officer and turned his attention to Mike.

"We've just about finished interviewing your flight attendants, the young man that assisted them, and a few of the passengers. I'll need to interview you and the first officer before you can leave."

During the entire time Mike had been on the tarmac, his internal "pilot" clock had been nudging him to get everything done that needed to be done and take off for Seattle as soon as possible. Sure, the crew was tired and hungry and one was a little roughed up. But he had spoken briefly with Karen, as he was making his way through the cabin, and she let him know, in no uncertain terms, that she wanted to continue the trip to Seattle.

Mike looked at his watch. It was early in the afternoon and this aircraft had a lot more flying to do before it was parked for the evening. Maybe he could work a deal with the FBI agent.

Mike said, "I need to get this aircraft moving down the line. How about this? You allow me to depart without further delay and I promise that Gary and I will both call you as soon as we get to the hotel in Seattle. You can have as much time with us as you want."

Agent Cauley thought about the offer for a second and then snarled, "You will call me as soon as you check in. No excuses. If you don't call, I will track you down. Understood?"

Mike gave his word that the agent could expect his phone call in approximately one hour thirty minutes, the estimated flying time to Seattle.

Agent Cauley offered his business card and the two men shook hands.

Utilizing a Great Falls police officer and his cruiser, Mike made a quick trip to the on-field FAA office to sign the dispatch release faxed in by the San Diego office. The dispatch release was the authorization from the company to resume the flight. Mike made it back to the aircraft just as the Flight Attendants were going through the safety briefing with the passengers. They were all back in their seats and appeared anxious to get home. As Mike strapped himself into the captain's seat, Gary informed him that he had completed the exterior inspection and everything looked fine.

In a voice that indicated his fatigue and, at the same time his relief that the ordeal was finally over, Mike said, "Very good, partner. Let's start the engines and get the hell out of here."

Saturday
1405 Central Standard Time

Pacifica Flight Seven Sixty-Two had been re-designated Pacifica Flight Seven Sixty-Two (Alpha). Since Gary made the landing in Great Falls, it was now Mike's turn to fly. Mike steered the aircraft perfectly down the center of the runway until take-off speed was reached. He smoothly pulled back on the yoke and the Boeing broke ground. Climbing through one thousand feet, Mike started a shallow right turn to intercept the course for Seattle-Tacoma International Airport.

The weather had improved significantly in the past hour and it looked like they would have clear skies all the way. The now familiar voice of the Great Falls controller came through his headset wishing the pilots a safe flight as he hands them off to Denver Center. Gary thanked the controller for his assistance and changed the radio to Denver's frequency.

Before he could check in with Denver, Mike raised his

hand to stop Gary. There was an ACARS message coming in. Both pilots stared intently at the screen as the following message was received:

> "TSA unable to complete review of passenger manifest prior to your departure from Great Falls.
>
> TSA/DEA confirms 2 drug fugitives onboard. Be advised that DEA bust planned upon your arrival in Seattle.
>
> Reply ASAP.

Mike and Gary glanced at each other and collectively shrugged their shoulders.

Oh, well.

Just another normal day of flying.

Epilogue

Captain Mike Rendell, First Officer Gary Ellis, and the three flight attendants, **Karen Schuhmacher, Sabrina Judson,** and **Michelle Timmons** were subpoenaed to appear at the trial of the hijacker. However, one week before the trial was to begin, both pilots were notified by the U.S. Attorney that they would not have to appear in court. The reason given for releasing the pilots was that neither of them had come in contact with the hijacker and, realistically, would not be able to identify him. Both pilots were asked to submit written statements to the court describing the events of that day according to their perspective.

The flight attendants, however, were informed that they would, definitely, testify in the trial of the hijacker. All three women flew to Great Falls only to be told, minutes before the bailiff was to call for order in the court, that the defendant had plead guilty to a lesser charge to avoid a jury trial. The flight attendants shook hands with the Federal attorneys and flew back to San Diego; landing in time to have lunch and congratulatory margaritas at a favorite

Mexican cantina.

Captain Mike Rendell is still a pilot with Pacifica Airlines, although he doesn't fly as much. His actions on May 24th earned him, and his entire crew, the company's "President's Award". Mike spends his non-flying days at Pacifica Airlines' pilot training center, where he instructs new captains in the areas of decision making and stress management. He and his wife, Lisa, also stay busy with their daughters. Both girls have developed an interest in sports – and boys. Both of these developments keep the Rendell family active – and Mike and Lisa wary.

First Officer Gary Ellis is now a Captain at Pacifica Airlines. His performance reviews are consistently above average and there are rumors that he may be "fast-tracked" to a Chief Pilots' position, possibly at the airline's new crew base – Portland, Oregon. Gary dated, and eventually married, the cute brunette that he danced with at the "Bombs Away Pub". He and his wife are the proud parents of twin boys.

Karen Schuhmacher completed the three-day trip without further incident. However, two days after returning home, she awoke in the middle of the night suffering from an anxiety attack. She had experienced a vivid nightmare that transported her back onboard Pacifica Flight Seven Sixty-Two; and into the clutches of her attacker. Karen and her husband spent the rest of the night discussing her experience that fateful day. The next morning, before the sun had fully broken the horizon, it was decided that her flying days at Pacifica Airlines had reached an end.

Today, Karen considers her misfortune an unexpected blessing. She went back to San Diego State University and updated her knowledge of the fashion industry. She and her husband opened a clothing store, not in the hustle and bustle of New York but, rather, in a wealthy enclave of Orange County, California. Her kids are older now and come by the shop, after school, to help their mom. Karen is prospering and, once again, having "fun".

Sabrina Judson remained at Pacifica Airlines for six months following the terror-filled day over Montana. Eventually, her husband convinced her that she should quit flying and they should follow their true spiritual calling. Today, Sabrina, now an ordained minister, her husband, and fifteen members of a non-denominational church live in the Amazon River basin where they assist with providing food, shelter, and clothing to the indigenous Indians. Every ninety days, Sabrina flies to the United States to visit family and her friends at Pacifica Airlines. During the six hour flight, she is constantly scanning the behavior of the passengers; trying to detect any subtle hint that trouble may be imminent.

Michelle Timmons, the perky blonde, still flies for Pacifica Airlines. Of all the flight attendants that worked Pacifica Flight Seven Sixty-Two, she seems to be the one least affected by the terroristic attempt on their lives. She married her pilot-boyfriend and they bought a house in San Diego which they share with their Old English sheepdog – Vector. Michelle and her husband try to fly with each other as much as possible. Occasionally, when she is away on a trip, Michelle will entertain the crew with her "butt quarter" trick. She still receives a standing ovation each time the coin "clinks" into the bottom of the glass.

Special Agent Frank Edward Cauley, of the Federal Bureau of Investigation, was commended for his actions in the apprehension of the hijacker of Pacifica Flight Seven Sixty-Two. The Director of the FBI transferred him to Washington, D.C. where Cauley acts as the liaison between the Bureau and the Transportation Security Administration's Federal Air Marshal Department. Although he enjoys his current responsibilities, Agent Cauley longs to return to the open spaces of Montana.

Leon Byford, a forty-five year old resident of Naperville, Illinois, was arrested and charged with the attempted hijacking of Pacifica Flight Seven Sixty Two. The charge is a Federal offense punishable by up to thirty years in a Federal penitentiary.   During his pre-trial evaluation it was determined that Byford's actions that day were the result of a drug related psychosis caused by severe heroin withdrawal. He subsequently pleaded guilty to a reduced charge of interfering with a flight crew member which is a Federal offense punishable by up to five years in a Federal penitentiary. Byford was released on bond while awaiting sentencing. Following his failure to show up at court for his sentencing, a bench warrant was issued for his arrest. The U.S. Marshals located him in Seattle, Washington and re-arrested him. He was charged with the additional crime of obstructing justice. Again, Byford was released on bond. Again, he did not show up at court for his second sentencing hearing. This time the U.S. Marshals located Byford in Seattle. He was brought back to Montana where the judge sentenced him to the maximum jail term possible – 5 years for the interference charge and twelve months for the obstruction charge. Byford appealed the court's ruling and the judge's decision was overturned by the Montana Court of Appeals due to a "sentencing guideline" mistake. The hijacker was given credit for time served – nine months.

He now walks the streets...a free man.

The Flight Continues!

About the Author

Captain Steve A. Reeves started flying airplanes from a dirt strip located adjacent to a cotton field in northeast Arkansas. He took great pride in his ability to chase rabbits down the plowed rows of the fields – and live to tell about it. However, it didn't take long for him to realize that chasing rabbits didn't pay very well. He packed his bags and headed to the University of Kentucky.

Upon graduating from college, he accepted a commission in the United States Navy. After one tour of duty, he thought that he'd had enough of flying and returned to the civilian world to pursue a career in construction management. One day while standing in the middle of a job site, Steve looked up in the sky to watch a commercial airliner fly over. The attraction was too powerful – he knew that he had to return to the sky.

Twenty-one years later, Steve has logged over 12,500 hours in civilian, military, and commercial aircraft. He is a captain for a major airline and resides in Texas with his wife, Stacy, and their two daughters, Keegan and Kayleigh.

Acknowledgments

I owe a special thanks to Bruce Moran. He suggested, four years ago, that I write this story. His support and guidance over the years has been invaluable. Thank you, Bruce. I couldn't have done it without you.

I am also grateful to Dr. Lucas "Luke" Boyd. Your friendship, sense of humor, and writing style is wonderful. I appreciate your honest and gentle critiques. Thanks, Luke, for helping me tell my story. There will be more to come.

And I am especially thankful for the love and support of my wife, Stacy. She is the inspiration for all that I do and all that I am.

Coon Dogs and Outhouses
Volume 1
Tall Tells from the Old South

This collection of his stories is part remembrance of a culture that is gradually fading, part recollection of lessons learned over a lifetime. Luke Boyd's matter-of fact style and clarity of detail are cut from the cloth of the oral tradition, which flourished in the rural South of his upbringing. He deftly places the hilarious story of chain saw-toting Phinos Ledbetter and his botched baptism at the East Fork Southern Missionary Baptist Church alongside the powerful memory of an uncle known by the poor tenant farmhands he served only as "The Jesus Doctor."

The author's characters are depicted so clearly and accurately as to leave the reader guessing which stories are fact and which are imagined. And whether the teachers in these tales are smudged with the dust of chalk or caked with the mud of the field, their lives and lessons are faithfully recorded here in the straightforward prose of Luke Boyd.

Title: Coon Dogs and Outhouses Volume 1

Author: Dr. Lucas G. Boyd

Publishing House: TotalRecall Publications, Inc.

Publication Date: 9/1/ 2008

ISBN Book: 978-1- 59095-837-7

ISBN eBook: 978-1- 59095-838-4

Coon Dogs and Outhouses
Volume 2
Tall Tells from the Mississippi Delta

Sometimes I stop and try to figure out where the stories come from and why I write the way I do. I'm sure much of it is a result of the land I grew up on and the people who were trying to scratch a living from it. One of my earliest memories is of a large fire in the middle of the cotton field. It was wintertime and I was helping Daddy burn chunks of stumps and roots which had accumulated during the crop season. It was a new ground farm only recently drained and released from the clutches of the brackish water of a Mississippi bayou. The soil was buckshot - rich, black, and grainy – unlike the light-colored, sandy loam of the old Delta. But the type of soil doesn't matter. If he stays in contact with it long enough, the land will brand a man as surely as the red-hot iron brands a Western calf. I'm sure the flat, almost treeless, bayou studded Delta of my early years which later was replaced by Mississippi's rolling, red-clay hills both placed their marks on me. My family had long been people of the soil and although I chose another profession, I have always been aware of the pull of the land.

Title: Coon Dogs and Outhouses Volume 1

Author: Luke Boyd

Publishing House: TotalRecall Publications, Inc.

Publication Date: 9/26/2008

ISBN Book: 978-1-59095-839-1

ISBN eBook: 978-1-59095-840-7